The Word Birds

God watches over all, especially our children. However, recently He's been dismayed as some of the children are not being taught the truth. So God called upon the Word Birds!

The Word Birds carry God's true word written on feathers beneath their wings.

Only a child has eyes to see this. Each time a child picks up a feather, God's truth is revealed in scripture.

Where are you going little birdie?
From where have you come little bird?

Can you visit for awhile?
Will you give me a true word?

Sing for me what's in your heart,
sing it loud and clear!

"Jesus Christ is Lord of all"
Sing for all to hear!

The truth will set you free.
John 8:32

Where are you going little children?
Where are you going precious one?
Which path will you follow?
Will you walk or will you run?

The word of God will guide your feet
wherever you may go.
The word of God will teach your heart
the things you ought to know.

He leads me in paths of righteousness
for his name's sake.
Psalm 23:3

I've been sent from the Father
delivering a treasure!

Is it silver?
Is it gold?

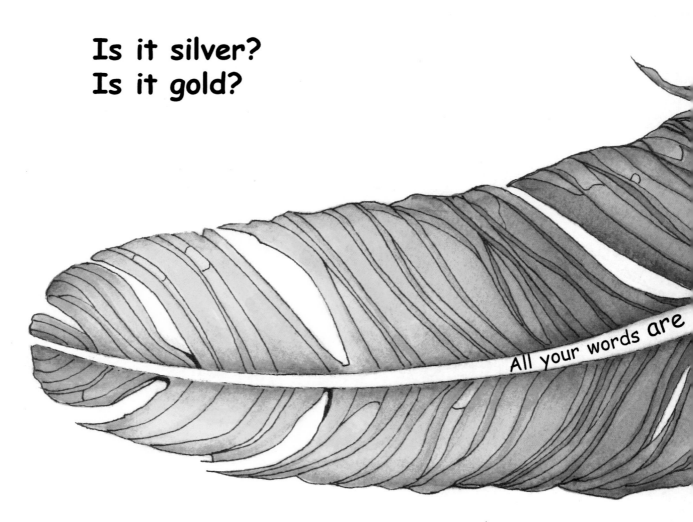

All your words are

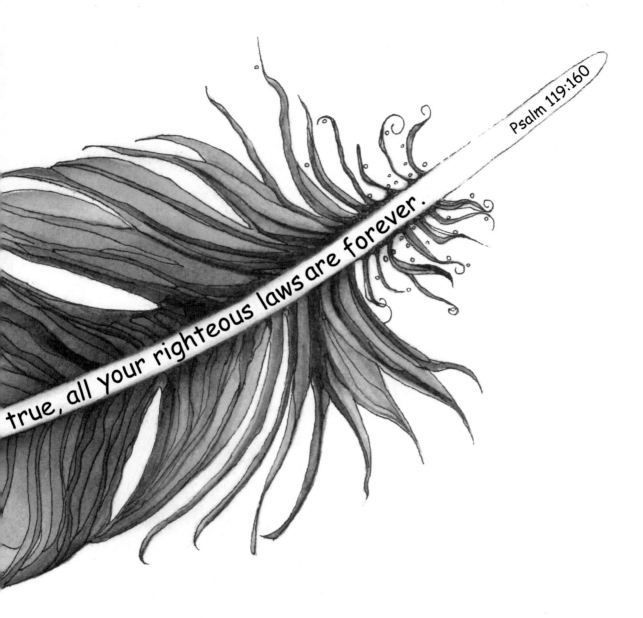

true, all your righteous laws are forever.

Psalm 119:160

'Tis truth upon a feather.

In a feather on the ground,
God's true word will be found.
Remember what your eyes now see,
for truth will never bend the knee!

The grass withers, the flower falls, but God's word stands forever. Isaiah 40:8

Jesus wants to dwell in your heart, rooted and grounded in love.

I am the way, the truth,

He is the way, the truth,
and the life. He is the light
from above!

and the life.

John 14:6

So, little children, walk in the light!
Chase the lies into the night!
Walk by faith not by sight!
Believe in Jesus with all your might!

For we walk by faith not by sight.
2 Corinthians 5:7

Remember children what you've heard,

delivered by a true Word Bird!

Stand firm then, with the belt of truth buckled around your waist.
Ephesians 6:14

THE WORD BIRD SQUAD

Jesus said, "Let the little children come to
me, and do not hinder them, for the kingdom
of heaven belongs to such as these."

Matthew 19:14

Eileen Onhim

Ima B. Liever

Carrie Mehome

Hal A. Looya

Will U. Follow

Phylis O. Spirit

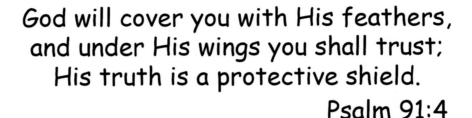

God will cover you with His feathers,
and under His wings you shall trust;
His truth is a protective shield.

Psalm 91:4

Dedicated to my beloved grandchildren Ava, Anson, and Eligh

Paperback ISBN: 979-8-9871071-0-2

Written and illustrated by Lorri VanLeuven

The Way Publishing - Fair Oaks Ranch, TX

All for God's glory

www.TrueWordBirds.com